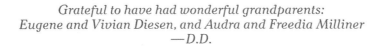

Grateful to have had wonderful grandparents:
Eugene and Vivian Diesen, and Audra and Freedia Milliner
—D.D.

For my good friend Jenny
—L.F.

Farrar Straus Giroux Books for Young Readers
An imprint of Macmillan Publishing Group, LLC
120 Broadway, New York, NY 10271

Text copyright © 2018 by Deborah Diesen
Pictures copyright © 2018 by Lucy Fleming
All rights reserved
Color separations by Bright Arts (H.K.) Ltd.
Printed in China by Toppan Leefung Printing Ltd., Dongguan City,
Guangdong Province

Designed by Roberta Pressel
First edition, 2018
10 9 8 7 6 5 4 3

mackids.com

Library of Congress Cataloging-in-Publication Data

Names: Diesen, Deborah, author. | Fleming, Lucy, illustrator.
Title: Hello, fall! / Deborah Diesen ; pictures by Lucy Fleming.
Description: First edition. | New York : Farrar Straus Giroux, 2018. |
    Summary: A grandparent and child recall the beautiful and wonderful
    sights and sounds of a fall day spent together.
Identifiers: LCCN 2017011333 | ISBN 9780374307547 (hardcover)
Subjects: | CYAC: Autumn—Fiction. | Grandparent and child—Fiction.
Classification: LCC PZ7.D57342 He 2018 | DDC [E]—dc23
LC record available at https://lccn.loc.gov/2017011333

Our books may be purchased in bulk for promotional, educational, or
business use. Please contact your local bookseller or the Macmillan
Corporate and Premium Sales Department at (800) 221-7945 ext. 5442
or by e-mail at MacmillanSpecialMarkets@macmillan.com.

Hello, FALL!

DEBORAH DIESEN

Pictures by
LUCY FLEMING

Farrar Straus Giroux
New York

Do you remember when we met that little woolly bear, making its way across the sidewalk? We stopped to say hello. We touched its gentle prickles and laughed when it curled into a ball.

We watched it uncurl and move on tiny feet through the sunshine and the shadows.

Squirrels were everywhere, digging holes and hiding acorns. We wondered: Would they remember all those spots later?

Around us we heard the whisper of trees.
Red leaves talking to yellow leaves talking
to orange leaves talking to purple leaves.

We listened closely, and then we whispered to
each other everything the trees had told us.

We sat on a big rock and crunched crispy apples and drank sweet apple cider. A flock of geese flew over and we waved up at them. They honked hello, so we pretended to be geese and honked back. Very noisily!

We touched our fingertips to the tiny petals of golden chrysanthemum blooms. We wondered if the mums were ticklish. We sure heard *someone* laughing!

Over in the pumpkin patch, we told a patient pumpkin all about our big plans. We found another pumpkin who was a good listener, too.

We picked them both, and we loaded them carefully.

We took turns pulling
the wagon home.

We liked it best when
we pulled together.

Back home, we both had the same
excellent idea about the leaf pile.
"Hello, fall!" we said as we ran
toward it. And fall replied,

"Jump in!"

Later on, we counted on our fingers all the bits of fall we'd said hello to. There were so many that we ran out of fingers, and we had to count on our toes.

When we did, we heard that wonderful laughter again!

Together, we savored the tender treasures
we'd found when we greeted fall:

BEAUTY,
BOUNTY,
WONDER,

And *LOVE*.